Billy's Wartime Fa

by

Paul Naylor

With acknowledgement to

Joan Brickley.

Val Carter.

Mary Gonzalez.

and

Silvia Gonzalez.

BILLY'S WARTIME FARM

WAS CREATED, INSPIRED

AND WRITTEN BY

PAUL NAYLOR

ILLUSTRATED BY

JOAN BRICKLEY

PREFACE

This book chronicles life and times on a wartime farm.

It follows the ups and downs of those people, who live and work on the farm, through the years of the Second World War.

In true British spirit, as their menfolk once again went off to fight the war and women took up the jobs left vacant, in both the factories and on the land.

The Auxiliary Territorial Service founded in 1917 was disbanded in 1921, but was reestablished in September 1939.

The Women's Land Army was also established during W.W.I and re founded in June 1939.

Initially the women were all volunteers,

however in December 1941 the government passed the National Service Act, allowing conscription for women into the armed forces, or for vital work in industry. By the year 1943 more than 80,000 women were working in the Land Army. Their tasks included, among many other things, milking, lambing, digging ditches, driving tractors and even catching rats, some 6,000 women worked as part of the Timber Corp, chopping down trees and working in the sawmills and woodyards.

Older women and those with young children, joined organizations such as the Townswomen's Guild, or the Women's Institute.

The W.I. were called upon to help with evacuees and rural food production. They also ran markets where surplus food was sold, at the other end of the scales, they provided knitted garments for army personnel at home or abroad. As the war got going the kind women preserved various food in jars and tins. The scarcity of oranges meant the scarcity vitamin C, which was only given to children. The W.I. helped other organizations to collect 500 tons of rose hips in order to make rosehip syrup, rich in vitamin C.

The Townswomen's Guild educated women to make their best contribution to the common good charitable activities and fundraising.

For the war would be fought on the home front, as well as in the field of battle, in foreign lands.

The government took over all walks of life, many grumbled, but as the war got going, the people accepted their lot and got on fighting the war, with a make do and mend policy.

Billy's Wartime Farm

Chapter One

Three months before I was to marry my fiancé Helen, my father became seriously ill, with my mother having died giving birth to me, and his only sister Betty, who had more or less raised me having passed away some eighteen months before, meant that he only had me to rely on. So, there was nothing else I could do but to move back to the farm to look after him, the land, and the livestock.

Thankfully, this did not mean that we had to postpone our wedding. My Helen, who was a kind person with a heart of gold, just two of the reasons why I loved her, said that she would move immediately into the farmhouse and help look after my father, thus making his last days as comfortable, and stress free as possible.

It was early in the summer of 1939 that we married, and sadly my father died just six weeks later. At that moment I found myself in complete charge of the farm, a funeral to arrange, and Mr. Hitler in Germany trying to make the whole of Europe his own. All three of these events made me feel that my free and easy days were numbered.

With the sad loss of my father, and the ominous news from the continent, I thought it a very sensible idea to try to organize, in advance, all things that could be organized. Not being a pessimist, just practical I bought the plot of land in the graveyard next to where my parents were buried. As I said to Helen, not wishing to be a prophet of doom, it was always best to try to think and plan ahead. If the worst came to the worst, then plans would be in place, if not needed, well then, life would be all the sweeter.

The farm, we had some five hundred acres, was on the outskirts of a village, halfway up the side of a mountain.

It looked westward, out over the north Wales coast. On a good day, you could see Ireland across the Irish Sea and Blackpool to the north.

Summers were glorious, but winters were bitterly cold and there were times when the farm was completely cut off by snow drifts.

Around this time, I think everyone knew that another war was inevitable, but to Helen's relief we both knew that I, as a farmer, would be exempt, together with the men that worked for me, always supposing they did not volunteer.

Many men from the village had already signed up and we felt that it would not be too long before the rest would follow, or be conscripted.

When war was finally declared, the last straw

of tolerance by our government being the

German invasion of Poland,

the village people went around with a sense of

here we go again.

In the first World War a great many of the

young men from the village and surrounding

countryside, who had marched away with a

certain sense of adventure, as well as pride, had died in the mud on the Somme, Ypres and in 'Flanders Field.' Many came home with life changing disabilities. No one wanted to go through that again.

But there we were, the country on high alert for invasion and once again men, and young boys who had to grow up quickly, were having to leave their homes and loved ones, to fight once again on foreign soil.

Although we were newly married Helen and I decided that, with the threat of bombing, air raids, or even invasion, we would put off having a family. All our waking hours would be needed to run the farm and produce food. We were well aware that as an island nation much of our food was imported, if the war went on for anywhere near the years of the first, we knew we would end up with shortages and rationing.

One evening, during the period which became known as the phony war, Helen and I took one of our usual evening strolls along the edge of the top fields overlooking the coast.

We looked out over the beach to the rolling

waves and watched soldiers laying down

barbed wire and other obstructions in order to

impede an invading army should they choose

to land there.

I tried to console Helen by saying that I

thought it very unlikely that German forces

would land in Wales, they were much more

likely to take the shortest route across the

English Channel from France, that is if they got

that far.

My thoughts at the time being only time would

tell.

Should the worst happen, and who knew at

that time just what would happen this time

around with all the newest armaments and

weaponry not to mention aircraft at Hitler's

disposal, I was content that I had prepared everything to the best of my ability, we just had to weather the coming storm and, God willing, we hoped it would all be over soon, how wrong we were.

I was glad, when I thought about it, that neither my mother nor my father had lived to see that day, but I did worry about Helen's parents who had been through all this before. Helen came from a large family and of course her brothers would be eligible for conscription. Personally, I had no worries in that respect, for my family was a small one and we only seemed to get together for births, deaths and marriages or as my father used to say   when a member of

the family was hatched, matched or

dispatched.

I would visit my parents grave often, and when

I did, I would sometime bump into the vicar of

St. James' Church, or someone from the

village.

On these occasions I became more aware that, as the dark clouds of war loomed, people seemed to become more chatty, nervous I suppose, seeking other people's company. As the days passed the villagers seemed to become closer, anticipating, well, they did not know what.

Billy's Wartime Farm

Chapter Two

As the phony war dragged on, I was kept busy
on the land and Helen had taken it upon
herself to learn to drive, which, she said you
never know, might be a handy thing to do.

I missed my father, but to help me with the day
to day running of the farm I took on a friend
named Ernie.

Ernie used to have a small farm nearer to the
coast but had sold it when his wife of twenty-
five years died and he had moved into a

rented cottage in the village. He had three sons, none of whom had been inclined to follow him on the land and had now signed up for the forces, two signed up for the army, and one for the Royal Navy.

Soon after all this I discovered that there were local council elections to be held and I wondered if I could serve the local people better as an elected councilor, I had asked Helen for her thoughts on the matter. She assured me of her full support if I decided to follow this path. She also suggested that I could ask Ernie to become my farm manager, thus freeing me up from most of my farming duties.

As the days of the war stretched into weeks, and it was becoming more and more obvious that the work on the farm would need more than a part time owner, I decided to forget my political career, at least for the time being. At this same time Helen also began to look for things to do in the way of helping in the war effort.

Not having children of her own she took to helping in the village school.

She also became an enthusiastic member of the newly formed W.I. in our area. One night whilst sitting by the fire, listening to one of our favorites, Tommy Handley, in his programme 'It mass,' I remarked to her that if her knitting needles went any faster, they would strike a spark. She smiled at me and knitted even faster.

Before long, people who could were asked to give a temporary home to children from the cities, we, having rooms to spare, put our names on that list. This became even more necessary when the Luftwaffe began systematically bombing the heavily industrialized cities. The nearest big industrialized cities to us were Liverpool and Birkenhead, prime targets being the docks and Cammell Laird's shipyards, not to mention the shipping convoys, that sailed in and out of the river Mersey.

'Early to bed, early to rise, makes a man healthy, wealthy and wise' is a well-known saying and there was going to be a lot of that early to bed and early to rise, because we all had to do as much as we could during daylight hours, I wasn't sure about the healthy, wealthy and wise bit.

Between the two wars there had been a lot of houses building just south of the village. One hundred and twenty-five new council properties had been built and occupied by the locals most in need, and a few families from further afield. This new influx had been a tremendous boost to the local economy. Many of the men found work in the pits, others at iron foundries, some took up farm work, but only as general labourers. Not many city dwellers knew anything about farming! But, all around, job vacancies were filled, and in many cases by the lassies.

My farm was running smoothly because even though I hadn't taken up my political career I still appointed Ernie as farm manager. He learned the working of the farm from A through to Z, it was always good policy to have a backup plan in case of a disaster.

 We both knew that food production had to be increased dramatically, even the orchard had to be improved upon to bring it to a better harvest, but I did not want to spend money on extra fruit trees as I felt that the extensive

farming of the land was going to dig deep into

our finances.

Whenever the government legislation for the

farming industry gave me a headache, I would

take myself off to visit mum and dad's grave. I

had, by this time, had a headstone erected

with a photo of each of them displayed on it.

So, whenever I felt completely stressed out, I

would take myself off to the graveyard

and enjoy the peace and tranquility I always

found there, and I would air all my anxieties or

grievances to my parents. Telling them all my

troubles never failed to make me feel better.

Occasionally I would meet the vicar, or the

verger, and they would fill me in on local news

not gossip though, never gossip. They would

just tell me what was happening, where and

why, because of the war.

Both of these people ended up being the most

unexpected of friends and one can ever have

too many friends.

Billy's Wartime Farm

Chapter Three

A blessing in the disguise of a young man named Martin who, having just reached the age of fourteen and having left school, came looking for a job at the farm. He said he would try his hand at anything if I would just give him a chance. I liked the look of him and so took him on at the sum of two shillings a week and told him he could live in the old cowman's hut, as part of his wages. The hut had just the basic amenities. Only cold water could be had from the kitchen tap, hot water must be boiled in a kettle on the small electric cooker. The place was furnished sparsely, but had curtains at the windows and rag rugs on the stone floors, these had been made many years before by my mother. There was also a comfortable bed in the separate bedroom. From a personal point of view, it was a comforting sight to see smoke once again curling out of the chimney from a fire, which I knew would be roaring away in the large black grate inside the old place.

I knew it would suit Martin until he reached the

age at which he could volunteer, if he wished

to, I knew he wouldn't be 'called up' because

land work was obviously, a reserved

occupation.

After Martin had settled in, we learned a little

more about him. He told us he came from a

large family and was grateful to have, not only a bed to himself, but two whole rooms as well.

We learned that he was a bright, intelligent boy, with a smile never far from his face. He would write home to his mum once a month and the villagers also got to appreciate his easy-going manner when he called into the village post office for a stamp. Martin reveled in his newly found freedom and Helen and I began to look upon him as the son, that we had not blessed with.

When he came to us, he had nothing, more or less, but the shirt on his back, but he soon put that right.

Whenever he heard of a jumble sale, off he would go.

This was how he acquired all he needed. He bought Nic nacs and other items to make his home cozy, as well as buying clothes for himself and of course, Helen had her knitting needles clicking for him.

He was also a dab hand with a stock pot, his mother had taught him well, he always had one on the go. A cup of tea and a bowl of broth were readily available to any of his visitors.

Winter was drawing in and Christmas would soon be upon us.

We decided to make the best of it, for who knew how many Christmases would come and go before this war was over.

That first Christmas, we invited Helen's sister, Pamela, to come to us for the holiday period. Whilst she was with us, we promoted her to chief organizer. She got stuck in with gusto, making many of the decorations herself from crepe paper, to hang in the church hall. She was a genius with wire coat hangers, covering them and tying balloons to them.

We obviously invited all our farm staff, and members of the church congregation, those who were unable to make it to the hall would have Christmas delivered to them.

The vicar, the Reverend Herbert Halliwell, was coming due for retirement but because of the now ongoing situation, he would stay on for the duration of the war, it was during this time that our friendship grew.

Helen and I, her sister and Herbert, all agreed that for the sake of the people in the community we ought to do our very best to put on a really good show, for who knew where we would all be in another twelve months' time.

Billy's Wartime Farm

Chapter Four

The Christmas festivities went down a treat, Pamela excelled herself. Everyone appreciated her efforts in her homemade decorations, the hall looked really festive. She even stuffed a Santa to sit in the corner, though most, good heartedly took the mickey and referred to this as Santa Fawkes or Scare Claus.

Having done our best at Christmas this was then followed by a rather quiet New Year's Eve for us on the farm.

As I looked out of the living room window Martin's hut was in darkness, for he had a busy day today and would have another one tomorrow, New Year's Day or not.

I turned on the radio to have it play softly in the background, while Helen and I sat together before a blazing fire in the hearth. We didn't talk about the future because that was in the hands of the good Lord, tomorrow well that was as far as we planned, so we just sat holding hands, enjoying the moment.

Just before midnight struck, I went outside into the farmyard carrying the traditional piece of bread and coal in my pocket.

Seeing the ships away in the Irish Sea, gave me just for a moment, a light sense of normality and a sense of hope. I saw the fishing trawlers sail out of Mostyn Docks for their first trip of the new year, wondering with dread if the U Boats would think that a fishing trawler was fair game in wartime. The thought of submarines sinking fishing boats sent a shiver down my spine and I changed the tack of my thoughts to the workings of the farm.

I had needed somewhere out of the way to collate all the extra necessary and unnecessary paperwork, that the government required to be completed, bureaucracy and red tape from the Whitehall boffins is the way I thought of it, but it had to be done so to this end, I had turned the small box room into a comfortable office, complete with a small radio so I could keep up with the B.B.C. news bulletins.

Helen was on the ball with the daily needs of the farm, so I had left many things in her capable hands.

As I continued to stand in the yard, oil lamp in hand, my thoughts turned to my father. He used to run the farm in a very efficient manner everything 'Ship shape and Bristol fashion' he used to say, but why he used a naval term for a working farm, I was never able to find out. But my father's ways were not my ways and I knew that in the current situation and in order to have things move forward, big changes had to be made, new year, new measures.

As midnight had struck and the boats out to sea were blowing their foghorns, I turned to knock on the farmhouse door. Helen opened it and from a small silver tray, she offered me a wee dram of whiskey, as I offered her the bread and coal, signifying the hope that our home would never be short of goodwill and joy.

I had 'let in the New Year' but with thanks to Mr. Hitler we did not expect it to be a good one.

Some of my workers had volunteered for the forces, so I would have to replace them. With the manpower shortage the replacements would have to be females. Land Army girls, who apparently would be able to look after livestock, plough the fields, drive tractors, and as I understood, mend them as well.

There was even a special Timber Felling Corp, I and others, were soon to find out just how good at their jobs these young ladies could be.

During the first few days of the new year, I had filled in all of the required questionnaires and statements now required by the government and had sent them off to my accountants.

This was a particularly quiet time of year for us, the farm would just be ticking over. With frost on the ground there wasn't much we could do apart from looking after the animals, generally tiding up and give a lick of whitewash wherever it was needed around the farmyard and outbuildings. A bit like the army saying if it moves salute it, if it's standing still, paint it. We had plenty of things standing still around the farm, with the farmhouse, the byres and the outbuildings, and plenty of limewash to cover it.

All were added to Martin's job description.

We had a heard of twenty-six dairy cattle from which we basically supplied the whole village with fresh milk, but I had plans to increase the herd, along with the poultry.

Money would have to be spent but this caused no problems, or sleepless nights, as there were funds in the bank and it would be an investment in the future of the farm. Everyone, family and farm workers alike, would all have to work together learning, lessons from the

First World War. We all knew that with

shortages, would come rationing and we also

knew that we would have to make do and

mend and to grin and bear it.

Billy's Wartime Farm

Chapter Five

We had two new arrivals on the farm, two legged ones, in the very trim shapes of Mary and Joan, Martin's twin sisters.

Martin had mentioned them some time before and said that his parents wanted somewhere safe for them, they were obviously thinking of the air raid situation. Helen and I agreed that they could come to the farm for we needed all the hands we could get. I had purchased an extra fifty cows when I had gone to the market town of Loppington, so we were desperately in need of more milk maids so, as far as we were

41

concerned, they arrived at just the right moment in time.

There would be no problems accommodating them, all we needed to do was make a few minor adjustments to the sleeping arrangements in the cowman's hut.

We put an extra single bed in the bedroom for the girls, and gave Martin a camp bed to sleep on in the kitchen.

Due to a government directive the farm had to get rid of the pigs, this apparently, was due to their excessive appetites, they were known as 'greedy feeders.'

When sold off the pigs, Ernie cleaned out the old piggery and after we had installed new boxes and drinkers and then we replaced the pigs with hens. This change meant that we would have a very good supply of eggs for ourselves and for the market.

We were blessed with good fortune as all the work on the farm, was moving forward without a hitch.

At the beginning of the farming calendar, I had ten thousand pounds in the bank, but as the farm expanded, taking on more because of the 'war effort,' the money was dwindling away,

but what choice did I have.

During the first full year of war, life moved at a

hectic pace, it was like living at a hundred

miles an hour, fields were tilled and crops were

sown, it was as though everything happened in

the blink of an eye, but with aching backs, we

just worked are way though the heavy work

toll.

In late summer, as the harvest became due,

we sent out a call for volunteers, for we

needed over and above the help and goodwill,

of the Land Army girls, that we already had.

Everywhere became a mad hive of activity and I was well aware of the hammering the bank balance would take with all the extra hands. Things were even more precarious money wise, because local customers were slow in paying their dues to us. Because of this I had not been able to pay anything into the farm account for two months and I needed the cash. The pressure was on to gather in the harvest, both from the land and my neighbour's wallets.

The farm was working at 'full tilt' and there were to be many long, hard days ahead of us.

It was, 'all hands-on deck,' to use another naval term.

We even had a few lads from a nearby army barracks help us out and believe me this was very much appreciated. Not to mention the fact that I did not have to pay them the army did.

It was one of the best harvests the farm had ever produced, but we all knew that in order to keep the country fed we, and other farms like ours, would have to keep on increasing the yield.

For seven long weeks we laboured and when all the produce had been stored away at a central collecting point at Loppington, only

then were we paid.

Billy's Wartime Farm

Chapter Six

As we entered the second year, things were at a standstill on the war front, 'though everywhere you looked on the home front was a hive of activity.

By this time the farm was financially stable even though I had spent substantial amounts on improvements.

Improvements meant better and quicker yields and easier working methods for the workers. A win, win situation I thought.

Going into the bank one day to deposit some cheques, I joined the rather long queue. Everyone was talking 'war talk' but I could not bring myself to join in any of those particular conversations.

Helen had asked me when I had finished at the bank if I would go on to the railway station and pick up a parcel for her. On my way I bumped into an old friend named Alf, a school friend from my youth, even he wanted to talk to me about news of his boys who were both in uniform and in France.

I commiserated with him in his anxiety, and commented on the many military personnel there were to be seen about these days, and

quickly moved on.

When I got to the station there was a train

standing at the platform disgorging refugees,

under the military precision of the leading

ladies of the W.I. I noticed that the majority of

these poor people were women and children,

there were not many men among them, and

those that were seemed either old or frail.

I later found out they were all from Poland.

To me they seemed to look frightened rather

than relieved that they had arrived at a safe

haven, perhaps they were still anxious about

loved ones left behind, plus not being able to speak our language. I secretly hoped no one would boggle their minds with Welsh even I still had trouble with that.

The refugees began the short walk to the church and village halls, where beds were awaiting them, while army trucks transported their meagre belongings. They were to be housed at the church and village hall temporarily, until they could all be moved on to the local people who had volunteered to put a roof over their heads.

As I had my truck with me, I offered the older people and those with small children a lift and discovered, from those who could speak English, that some of them already had young relatives in the Royal Airforce, some as pilots' others as navigators or even ground crew. These 'new' people in the village, would in some ways, change our lives in more ways than one before the war was over.

On my return I came across Martin in the yard who offered me a bowl of broth he had simmering on the stove, this was a most welcome offer I told him, as Helen had not yet returned from whatever she had gone off to do, she wasn't at the station with the ladies of the W.I., organizing refugees.

Martin liked visitors, so he always tempted callers at the farm with a tasty bowl of broth, and who could resist a nourishing bowl of goodness after a day, or even just a few hours, hard graft.

The cowman's hut became a focal point for the farm labourers when they were off duty, so to speak, I particularly enjoyed his company for his wide diversity in subject matter. For a young man, Martin was very well read and his varying interests were a distraction from the

blessed war.

Billy's Wartime Farm

Chapter Seven

They say things happen to offset each other, a good event followed by a bad, or the 'other way round.

The good event was that we were asked to look after, foster, three young boys. These brothers, bless them, had travelled from Liverpool, chaperoned by a member of the W.I., Mrs. Amelia Osborne.

A visit that Helen had, apparently, been finalizing when she went missing the day of the arrival of the Polish refugees.

Mrs. Osborne told us that the boys' father had died on the beaches of Dunkirk and their mother had been killed in a bombing raid on Liverpool and as far as they knew there were no other family members to look after the poor little mites.

Although Helen and I had made the decision not to bring any children of our own into this war torn world when we were approached with this sad story, how could we refuse to keep these three orphans in our safe keeping.

So, Alfie, Georgie and Bobby, the three brothers, were the good thing that happened. The sad thing to happen was that Bert Ollerenshaw passed away.

Bert was a long-term friend of my father and farmed the land next to ours, he was a much loved and very respected member of the village community, and many would feel his sad loss.

With her husband's death, his widow, Doris, decided that at that point in her life she would retire from her job as housekeeper at the vicarage and let someone else take on the work. There were plenty of people around for the vicar to choose from, even from among the Polish residents, all of whom were settling into country ways very nicely.

Doris, having no one to pass the farm on to, allowed me to make an offer for the land, which she duly accepted and it became part of my domain, while she looked for a cozy little bungalow to buy and move into.

When I'd lost my father Bert, Doris was a tower of strength to me, now was the time for me to return that kindness by supporting Doris in her hour of need.

Doris had worked at the vicarage for more years than anybody cared to remember and it was thought that giving her a retirement party would be a nice gesture. However, under the circumstances, Helen and I, with the agreement of the vicar, decided that anything

we did do, would have to be postponed until

she had recovered a little from her sad loss.

When the event finally did take place,

everyone said what good time they'd had.

Planned as just a get together it had turned

into a right good knee up, just what everyone

needed, and it was so good to catch up with

old friends and share family news and village

gossip.

As Helen and I left the hall that night, before

we headed home, we took a stroll along the

narrow country lane that ran parallel to the

church and hall. We walked to the top where

the moonlit vista stretched out before us, there

we sat, on a stonewall, quietly holding hands.

We felt at peace with ourselves until, as we

looked over the water to our right, we could

see the dark night sky lit up, as though all the

Guy Fawkes nights had rolled into one. It was

the blaze from incendiary fires   Liverpool and

Manchester were the main targets, once

again, for the German bombers.

 As we looked on in horror, not being able to

even imagine the hardships, pain and anguish,

the sheer terror and devastation that the

people of those towns were facing on that

night, going down into air raid shelters to avoid

the bombing not knowing when they emerged,

whether their homes would still be standing.

Thinking of the three boys back at the farm,

and what they had lost, our hearts went out

across the dark miles which separated us and

those horrendous scenes across the water,

and we both silently thanked God for what we

had, which seemed a bit selfish, as though we

were thankful it was them and not us.

We wished it was none of us.

We knew there was nothing we could do to

ease their pain and suffering, but we made this

vow that we would do all we could, the only

way we knew how and that was to fight our

war on the land, producing as much for the

war effort as we possibly could and keep

everyone in our prayers.

 We prayed especially for those R.A.F. fighter

pilots that we could see taking off from the

base not far from the farm, flying off to who

knew where, into who knew what danger.

 We stopped counting how many planes would

take off from the base, because it was too

upsetting not to count the same number

returning so many young men lost.

As we continued to sit, we discussed the plight

of the three orphans in our care. No other

relatives had been found which meant that

when the war was over, they would have to go

to an orphanage or someone might adopt

them, but would someone adopt all three and keep them together. Siblings were more often than not split up. With that thought going through our minds as we came to the same decision almost at the same minute   What about us.

So far, we had no children, the boys already loved the farm and we had proved that we could accommodate all three of them so, why not us. If at some later date we were blessed with children of our own, they would be lucky enough to be apart of a family and have some younger sibling.

We would have to put the wheels of bureaucracy into motion, for from experience, I knew they moved exceedingly slow.

Life on the home front did not get any easier. As food shortages began to take hold, rationing was introduced. Fortunately for us on the farm we could nearly always produce a little extra meat for our dinner table as rabbits abounded in the area.

But along with the bad news there was a little good. We had been allocated a tractor with all the necessary implements needed to go along with it, what a labour saver. So much so that I put my name down for another one, nothing

ventured, nothing gained.

Billy's Wartime Farm

Chapter Eight

The war just dragged on and on.

On the news we heard that the invasion of
Russia by the Germans had come to a halt.
The subzero winter temperatures, which the
German troops were unused to, plus the
determination of the Red Army, had stopped
any further hope that Mr. Hitler had of
subjugating Russia as he had subjugated
many other countries in Europe, which had
started this whole sad business. He got away
with a bit here and a bit there, until he was told
no more, but he got too greedy.

However, the most momentous piece of news, came just before Christmas of that particular year 1941. We heard that the Japanese Airforce had, without warning or declaration of war, bombed Pearl Harbour, the American Naval Base on Hawaii in the Pacific Ocean.

This act made the American President Roosevelt declare war on Germany as well as Japan as they were allies of each other. With this extra fighting power, we, on the home front, all felt that maybe, just maybe, this was the beginning of the end of hostilities.

There was a wind of change all around us.

The air raids over Liverpool were lessening but

the rationing was getting tougher.

Another neighbouring farmer decided to give

up and sell up, so I stepped up again and

bought all one hundred and fifty acres, this

would be the last addition I was to make to my

'domain.'

At this point I had the largest farm in the area,

but I had ploughed all my savings into the

business, I had to make a success of it to

replace my almost, nonexistent, bank balance.

The importation of food had now fallen to an all-time low. The German wolf packs, the U Boats, were making quite a success of intercepting our Merchant Navy convoys sailing across the Atlantic, and were sinking ships loaded with much needed supplies, so it was imperative that the home farms produce more than ever, good harvests were imperative.

Everyone in the country felt the wrench whenever we read of yet another Merchant ship, or Royal Navy escort vessel being sunk. Food and much needed supplies were lost, yes, but the loss of life did not bear thinking about.

We plodded on and thankfully, had a good harvest and having expanded the dairy herd our milk yield was up and were also at that time, able to send fifty-two beef cattle to the slaughter house.

We had also sold off the extra farmhouse and buildings on the farms that I had bought. All this meant we were able to add to the coffers, taking us out of the red and into the black at the bank, thus putting a smile on the bank manager's face.

I don't think he had much else to smile about during those hard days, he too, like many others had a son in the forces. His was now fighting in the desert somewhere in North Africa.

During the following years many things changed, but none more so than having American military personnel stationed in England's 'green and pleasant land' as they say. We didn't meet up with many of them in Wales but we certainly heard their type of music over the wireless   jitterbug and jive music   plus, among others, the big band of Glenn Miller who was entertaining the troops both in England and in Europe with his 'In the Mood,' 'String of Pearls,' and 'American Patrol.' I have to say that Helen and I were quite taken with the 'Big Band Sound.'

Just a few years after they had first arrived, we heard rumours of gatherings on the south coast, something big was in the air.

Then it happened, Operation Overlord, they called it D Day.

It was the 6th June 1944, the allies invaded France, landing on the beaches of Normandy, the Second Front had begun, surely the end of this dreadful conflict was in sight.

Everyone was buzzing with the news but, I noticed, Martin wasn't and I didn't understand why. I called Ernie into my office and asked if he knew why Martin was so downcast. Ernie told me that Martin had received his call up papers and while he was resigned to 'doing his bit' as others had before him, he was very unhappy at leaving his sisters and the farm. Later in the day I looked in on Martin to have a talk with him. Martin told me he was happy to go but was worried about his sisters. I told him that there was no problem, Joan and Mary could stay on the farm in his cowman's hut and keep the 'home fire burning,' until he returned. I made him promise that he would return to the farm after the war, whether he would want to take up his work again would be a different matter.

We had a little 'get together' for the farm workers to wish Martin, Godspeed. The following day Helen and I drove him to the station. After Helen hugged him tight, she made him promise not to forget to write to his sisters.

As we stood on the platform, waving the train from the station, we both felt as though we were saying goodbye to a dear brother, rather than an employee.

Billy's Wartime Farm

Chapter Nine

Time can change everything, add a war to that

and everything changes even more.

The village that I grew up in now seemed a

memory, for with the addition of refugees,

Land Army girls and those taking refuge in the

countryside from the bombings of their towns,

the village was now more or less a town,

although it be a small one.

How I missed the slower prewar days, as

I continued to miss Martin.

Wanting some time alone, I wandered up to the graveyard to visit my parents grave, to moan all my worries away to them. I pointed out to them all the fresh graves that had been dug, some of them war graves of fresh-faced young men, who would never grow old and one of a young lassie I noticed, who had apparently got caught up in some shelling whilst attending to the wounded, a member of the Queen Alexandra's Nursing Corp. She was the daughter of one of the old established families of the village, I knew them well and my heart bled for them in their loss.

'So many,' I said to the vicar, when I called in to see him. 'So many who would not come home, so many families that would never be the same.'

There were even graves that held the bodies of German airmen. Their plane had been damaged by the anti-aircraft guns, while it was taking part in a raid on Liverpool. The pilot had managed to fly over the River Mersey and the River Dee but had lost altitude and crashed into the Welsh hills.

Items, proving the identity of the crew, were taken from the wreck and the bodies, to be kept until after the war and returned to their families, for although they were the enemy, they were still some mothers' sons. It was the Christian thing to do.

My earnest prayer, as I walked through the cemetery, was that this really would be the war to end all wars.

It would seem that the good Lord was on our side that year as we had a bumper harvest. Every part of the farm was being utilized, even the hedgerows.
Because of the German U Boats   oranges from abroad were never seen, not by us anyway, this meant that children would be

lacking in vitamin C, so the ladies of the W. I.

set about collecting berries for the making of

Rose hip syrup as a substitute.

 The hedges around our farms were also full of

blackberries and there were locals growing

raspberries and gooseberries all good for

making jam. Nothing was to go to waste,

everything was either make do or mend, it

became the village watch word,

 everything that could be recycled was.

The farm was working at full tilt, everything

that we produced went into the central

collecting warehouse in Loppington. The

Ministry of Food was doing a great job.

I had a milking machine installed to increase

efficiency, because of this the twins were not

needed for the milking as they had been in the

past, but they still kept their hand in, so to

speak, for the few cows that could not make

the change. Apart from that there was always

plenty for them to turn their hands to,

 they helped the Land Army girls with their

tasks.

The Land Army girls, to whom I owed a great

debt, a debt I could never repay in full, for

without their hard work and diligence we would

never have been able to achieve all that we

had achieved.

I never believed that they received the

accolades they were entitled to. Men went

away to war, while women fought at home

front, helping to keep the factories and the

farms running, and keeping homes together.

Billy's Wartime Farm

Chapter Ten

The winter of '44/45 was a bad one, and rationing was at its toughest yet.

You had to look after what you had as there was nothing spare.

On the farm we counted ourselves lucky, we were better off than most, we wrapped up well as we carried on about our business. Helen's knitting of scarves and mittens came in very handy and I appreciated the extra warmth of a knitted sweater.

Most of the livestock were safe, they were in shelter, the calving sheds were full, and all of the ewes were pregnant.

Under the new pig share programme, we had been allocated twelve pigs and the farm would get its share when they were divided up.

The milk lorry kept on going, ice or no ice on the roads, the driver did a stalwart job.

The large hen sheds were at the maximum of production. We had introduced a breeding programme to keep the numbers up.

Powdered eggs were the order of the day for most people, a fresh egg was an unknown luxury, unless the person kept the odd chicken

in their backyard or garden.

  The sale of eggs was at a premium and we

made a steady income from them, but did not

charge extortionate prices as some people did.

There was always roast chicken on the table

for Sunday lunch, which sadly did not go far

when shared between seven of us, Mary and

Joan, the three boys, Alfie, Georgie, and

Bobby and Helen and I,

good job Martin wasn't there as well.

We had twenty-two working horses on the

farm to do various jobs, ploughing, harvesting,

tilling, making deliveries, they were the

backbone of the farm. My head horseman,

Gerry, was the best in the business, or so I

thought 'til I saw the Timber Girls, they opened

my eyes.

 Those Timber Girls worked as hard, if not

harder than any man I had ever seen and the

horses in their charge were well trained and

therefore well behaved. They were part of the

Land Army and were overseen by the Forestry

Commission, they took charge of every aspect

of the felling of the trees and the running of the

sawmills, I never needed to check up on these

girls.

Because of the horses the local blacksmith was a regular visitor, checking and reshoeing the horses when necessary. He was also capable of mending any of the farm's metal implements whenever they were in need of repair, which all added to the farm's outgoings.

As well as looking after the three boys Helen had, from the beginning, taken on the lion's share of the office work. There was no way I could have coped with all that paperwork as well.

Behind every man there's a good woman.

Another Christmas came and went and

everything still looked bleak, after the

excitement of D Day the war still seemed to be

dragging on, perhaps those of us who were

nowhere near the fighting thought it would all

be over in days. What did we know, at least we

tried our best to make it a pleasant time for the

children.

Something that did happen, was the death of

the popular American band leader, Glenn

Miller. We heard about it from a wireless news

bulletin on Christmas Day. It was reported that

on the day before, Christmas Eve, he had

boarded a plane to fly to Europe in order to

give a concert for the troops, when the plane

he was flying in disappeared over the English

Channel.

Poor Mrs. Glenn Miller.

It didn't matter who you were, rich or poor,

famous or otherwise, this war brought

heartache and sadness to all walks of life.

Our hearts went out to her and all the relatives

of the people on that plane.

We had all learned many times over the past

four or five years that war, apart from bringing

devastation and destruction to towns and

homes, can devastate people's lives, homes

and surrounding area.

Billy's Wartime Farm

Chapter Eleven

On more than one occasion the country had come dangerously close to running out of food, and although we felt that the end of the war was in sight, the farming communities still had to carry on working as hard as ever.

Helen and I were both of the same opinion, that rationing books would still be with us for some time yet to come, even long after the war had ended. So farm workers just had to keep going with their 'heads down', as they say.

We were obviously as much a part of the war as the soldiers, sailors, and airmen, but the war on the farm was a silent war, no one ever complained, they just got on with the job in hand.

One of the novelties of the war was the training of the members of the Home Guard. We had watched them when they used our outer pasture land for drilling purposes, each man with a wooden rifle angled on his shoulder, as a member of the regular army. Sometimes a retired officer of the 'old brigade' would be shouting orders at them.

Maneuvers could be hilarious to watch, they'd

spread dirt on their faces and crawl on the

ground, learning how to sneak up on the

enemy. These things did look silly to us at the

time, but we were more than aware that at the

beginning of the war, when no one knew what

would happen, as England stood alone against

the Germans, these volunteers of the Home

Guard could have been a vital cog in the

defense of the realm. Nobody wanted to under

rate the contribution played by the over one

million men that volunteered

Many of these men were to continue in their

silent war, but this time it was the war on want

by working on the farms after their units had been stood down and disbanded.

Wars change everything and people's lives change forever.

It was the same for us on the farm, new methods, new equipment had been installed as a matter of necessity and there was no going back, indeed, it would have been foolish to return to old ways and who wanted too anyway. It stood to reason that with all the new labor-saving devices and new ways, production had escalated over the years. 'Needs must when the devil drives,' as my granny used to say.

As spring arrived that year a new sense of optimism arrived with it. The talk changed from will we win the war to when we win the war.

With no one giving us a date for the cessation of hostilities we carried on working as hard as always. We found that many of the Land Army girls were thinking about the time when they would have to leave the farm, but I assured them that I felt that that time was still a long way off. Some of them even began to make enquiries about future, permanent employment on the farms. Hard work or no hard work, some of them had come to love life on the land.

Billy's Wartime Farm

Chapter Twelve

During the war years many people had to grow up quickly, young teenage boys having to go off and face whatever horrors awaited them on the battlefield, which led us to think of Martin.

Before he had gone away Martin had made a will and asked Helen and I to be his executors, which we had readily agreed to, we saw it as wise precaution under the circumstances.

Martin had written to his sisters as often as he could, and he always put a little note for us in the same envelope.

His latest message made me stop and think.

Helen and I now had the future of three boys to think of so we needed to take a leaf out of Martin's book we needed to remake our own wills.

We left the children in the capable hands of Mary and Joan and took a ride into Loppington.

The original idea was just to visit our solicitor and have him amend our Last Will and Testament, but, as we had not been able to have a honeymoon, I decided to treat Helen to three days in a reasonable clean hotel in Loppington, but at least it did the job.

Three whole days of not having to think about yields or quotas. "Bliss," said Helen.

Although I was still rather a young man the war years had taken its toll on me. How many years would I be able to work at the rate I had been working. Fortunately for us, the good Lord had been generous to us in bringing Alfie, Georgie, and Bobby into our lives and hopefully they would grow up loving the land as much as I did and want to take it over from me, so far, the signs were good.

We had already witnessed the boy's love of farm life.

When there was an orphan lamb there was a fight as to who would get to bottle feed it. We had so many broken eggs when they fought over who was going to collect them until Helen made out a Rota.

But the greatest joy came to us when the boys called us mum and dad on the day, we told them that the bureaucratic wheels had finally stopped in our favor they were now officially our sons.

As the news from all fronts of the war in Europe were being transmitted, we eagerly awaited the final words victory was ours.

Parties were being planned all over the country, everyone scraping together what they could.

Flags were being dug out of cupboards, bunting was being made and bells church bells which had been silent for so long would ring out again across the countryside.
Our local Peel Society had been reformed and waited eagerly for the 'nod' from the vicar.

Every person in the whole country was just

waiting for 'Winnie's' (the Prime Minister's)

announcement.

Then, at last it came, we could unglue our ears

from our radios. On Tuesday 8th May 1945,

Victory in Europe was declared.

V. E. DAY at last.

The peelers, all over the country, rang their
church bells with gusto, this included our own
local campanologists.

It was the signal for the street parties to
begin.

Conga lines that formed went on for miles, as
people, drunk and sober, tagged on to the end,
and how many times we did the 'Hokey Cokey'
I will never know.

Sadly, amidst all this celebration there was still
sadness, for this was not the end of the war, it
was only the end of the war in Europe. There
were still many brave people fighting in the far

east, and many more who, thinking their war was over, would be re deployed to help them.

V.J. Day, Victory over Japan, was, although we did not know it at the time, still some four months away.

Billy's Wartime Farm

Chapter Thirteen

After the celebrations for the victory in Europe things more or less returned to how they were during the hostilities. Rationing continued on the home front and the war dragged on unmercifully in the far east. The country was bankrupt, but the farm thankfully was in a good state of solvency.

The worst thing on our horizon was worrying about Martin. The twins had not heard from him for some time, so we did not know where he was, or how he was, whether he would manage to come home on leave, or sent like many others, to finish the war against Japan. The third option did not bear thinking about. Helen absolutely refused to contemplate that Martin had been killed, we had no notification or even a notice of 'missing in action' so she clung on to the old saying that 'No news is good news.', what more could we do.

One thing that didn't change immediately was the employment of the Land Army Girls, especially the Timber Girls, for this we were truly thankful. We knew that once the men, I had been demobbed from the forces many would want to return to their old jobs, but with the new mechanization and the Land Army girls this would pose a problem. The modern equipment was quicker and more efficient than men were and some of the 'Girls' did not want to go back to their city lives after their years on the farm.

What a quandary to be in as an employer, what a headache.

Part of that headache was solved for me, in a way I wished that it had not.

Eight of my farm lads who had signed up, had been killed in action, a few more were noted as 'missing' and a few more had signed up for the Regs, the Regular Army. After seeing

foreign countries, even under the most horrific

of circumstances, they did not want to be tied

down to the hard life of a farm labourer again.

They much preferred a life of being told what

to do twenty-four hours a day. When to eat

and when to sleep. Not to mention free board

and lodgings and a pension at the end of it.

Plus, when this war was finally all over, they

thought, perhaps they would be on a 'cushy

number' training for war, but with no war to

go to. A bit like a football team training for a

cup final but never taking part in a match at

Wembley.

Little did they know that in just over five years from V.E. Day, there would be another war for them to fight in Korea, a place that probably most of them had never heard of, so not a cushy number then at all.

With a certain amount of irony, as the sums worked out, sad to say, the casualties of the war culled my farm workforce numbers sufficiently so that the headache I had expected did not arise.

Time marched on, as it always did and finally victory over Japan.

The Japanese it seemed had wanted to fight until 'last man, last bullet' we heard that many of their troops committed suicide rather than surrender. When we heard this Helen and I were both of the same mind, what kind of mind set did these people have?

The Americans wanted an end to hostilities as quickly as possible and end the loss of American lives.

With this aim in mind the American President sanctioned the dropping of two bombs on two of Japan's main towns, Hiroshima and Nagasaki. Bombs the like of which we had never seen before, with the most horrendous and catastrophic results on the people. Only after this did the Japanese Emperor and generals finally admit defeat and submit. They came aboard the American warship U.S.S. Missouri, anchored in Tokyo Bay, for the signing of the surrender documents, the date was the 2nd September 1945. The surrender documents were then handed over to American General, Douglas MacArthur. General MacArthur had seen plenty of action in the Pacific and was the Supreme Commander, Southwest Pacific, this seemed like a reward for all his dedication, determination, and leadership.

Please God we prayed that that was the end

of all the hardships

of war.

Sadly, we heard that the repatriation for

prisoners of war was a slow and painstaking

process, consequently many died after the

peace, never making it back home and sad to

say that many of those who did get home were

'broken' almost beyond repair having spent

years working in the Japanese labour camps.

Billy's Wartime Farm

Chapter Fourteen

The ending of the conflicts brought both joy and sadness in equal measure for some.

On our own 'door step' nice things happened. Both of the twins, Mary and Joan, had married. Joan had actually married one of the Polish men who had come over on the refugee transport, his name was Pavel, a very kind, polite and hardworking young man, a little older than Joan but no one minded that, they seemed made for each other. The reason he had been on the transport was that he was

unacceptable for combat. The Polish Army
had classed him as disabled, but Joan said he
was not disabled, he was just unable to do
certain things, but he was a brilliant
woodcarver and hoped to start his own
business.

Mary had met an American airman, who had
asked her to marry him. Mary was more than
delighted to say yes but with one reservation
she did not want to go and live Stateside, as
the Americans called it. She wanted them to
live in Wales. She could not bear the thought
of leaving her twin.

So, it was settled   the 'Yank' who had fallen
in love with the Welsh countryside, as well as

Mary, was happy to oblige and they looked around for land they could buy, he fancied trying his hand at raising horses, maybe racing them he said.

Apparently, Americans were loaded with money, or so it seemed.

The marriages of Mary and Joan meant that the cowman's hut   Martins place   was now standing empty, so I offered it to Ernie, who could have retired, but decided he wasn't ready to be put out to pasture just yet.

We would often reminisce of days before, and during, the war whilst sitting in front of the log fire in his place, sharing a glass of stout, our thoughts inevitably turning to Martin.

We wondered just what had happened to him and whether, when the years had passed, his sisters would have him declared officially dead, that is if the War Office did not give them satisfactory answers in the meantime.

Meanwhile our own little world was changing. The eldest of our adopted boys, Alfie, had joined the Army. We were so proud of him when, home on leave, on the 11th November 1948, he stood beside us during the Service of Remembrance at the local Cenotaph, remembering 'All those who would not grow old.'

We all gave our thoughts to Martin, although the War Office had been in touch with the twins and told them that Martin was officially missing, presumed killed in action. Not a part of him had been found, no 'dog tally,' nothing. Under these circumstances Helen still hung on in faith that Martin was out there somewhere, but why he had not come home she could only guess, loss of memory maybe, more than this she could not say.

To keep his memory alive, I had a wooden plaque, beautifully carved by Pavel, placed in the porch of our village church with Martin's name on it and an inscription which read

'Lost and never found.'

And we carried on living in slender hope.

Close to home, the village of Tindale had now

grown into a town. Pre-fabricated houses

were springing up so quickly, all over the

place. These, pre made in the factory,

houses, were the government's answer to the

problem of putting a roof, very quickly, over the

heads of those who had been bombed out of

their homes and of those who had not been

bombed out, but wished they had, from their

overcrowded, damp, moldy, rat infested, living

accommodation.

No one in their right minds could have, by any

stretch of the imagination, called them homes.

With the extra housing came extra people, this

meant everything else had to increase to keep

pace, shops, schools, transport facilities, and

health care, for the summer of that year,1948

we saw the dawning of something called the

National Health Service. People were told they

would be looked after from the cradle to the

grave, the latest political slogan.

The new occupants of the pre fabs came from far and wide. People who did not mind leaving town life behind.

At first the ways of the country folk clashed with those of the 'townie' but eventually all came together to live in harmony. For the most part anyway, though there would always be the odd one who has no wish to conform, which is fine, just so long as they didn't cause trouble, Constable Owens, Tinford's local policeman, was used to a rather quiet, easy going, kind of life.

Having a healthy bank balance, I purchased some more land, which the Council had put up for sale. It had been commandeered by them, for the war effort and now they simply did not need it after all and sold it on.

Our farm now consisted of two and half thousand acres, plenty big enough for Helen and I.

The mechanical innovations which had been introduced during the war years were now a necessity for the acreage we owned and a double bonus in our lives was that we had no debts.

Billy's Wartime Farm

Chapter Fifteen

During the winter of '48/'49 it was beyond being bitterly cold, it was one of the worst we had seen in living memory, everybody suffered. There was even ice on the inside of the windows, but thanks to the Lumber Girls we still had a stock pile of timber and were able to maintain a fire 'round the clock.

To add to the general population's misery, rationing was still in force, with no end in sight.

Just when we thought the winter would go on forever, but spring slowly arrived. The thaw was gradual, and temperatures were still a little less than they would normally have been, but, newborns, be they lambs or calves, wait for no man.

The cycle of farming was going round again. We needed to get livestock to the markets to sell in order to pay for necessities.

These necessities also included paying our mortgage.

Helen and I had done our sums years ago profits from the dairy herd paid the mortgage, profits from the rest of the farm paid for everything else. We had some years prior to this, invested in the buying of some beef cattle, which, though a good addition to the farm, and I had no regrets at my decision, would take sometime to show an advantage in the profit margins.

The value of our well-run farm increased, the buildings, land and livestock. The mortgage, thankfully, remained the same.

We had to concentrate on our finances very carefully for what came in seemed to be spoken for, or allocated to some new scheme, such as the six new Dutch barns we had built.

These barns were a new innovation, especially designed for the storing of hay, straw and animal feed. The unique design of these Dutch barns, named so because they were thought of and designed in Holland, reduced the risk of fire, simply because of the especially built in air ducts which allowed air to circulate thus keeping the stacks cool, therefore reducing the risk of them smoldering and catching alight.

Billy's Wartime Fam

Chapter Sixteen

The day came when Ernie felt he had earned his retirement. He wanted to go, he said, while he still had some life left in him to pursue, among other things, a gentle widow lady he had met at a tea dance which was held at the ex-servicemen's club in Loppington, and to which end, he had bought a small terraced house.

He also had this itch, he said which he had been unable to scratch until now, and that itch was Martin. He wanted an answer to the mystery of Martin.

Ernie himself was a gentle soul, but when he got a bee in his bonnet, nothing could detract him from his 'quest.' He had established a close bond with Martin, as I had myself, but he now had the time, as I never would, at least not for years to come, to go and dig into finding answers to unanswered questions, and if there was a grave, he wanted to find it.

Being the quiet person that he was, Ernie just moved out without any fuss. He said that he did not want a celebration of any kind and was adamant that he did not want the proverbial gold clock on his leaving. On the matter of the latter, Helen and I put our heads together and decided that we would wait until Ernie and his gentle widow lady tied the knot, for Helen an incurable romantic, was quite certain that they would, and then we would buy them a nice, mantle carriage clock for their new home. My wife is an extremely practical woman.

I could almost see into the future of the farming industry, and it was a very different industry from that which I had known as a lad.

When a member of staff, such as Ernie left, they weren't being replaced, it was a sign of the times, as mechanization was coming to the fore.

My thoughts turned to myself; how long would I feel that I wanted to follow the farming life I had always known.

Farming was in decline like me, though I knew that I was not over the hill, nowhere near it, but like Ernie I also knew there was more to life which Helen and I had missed.

Children of our own had never materialized, but we both felt that we had not missed out. We both believed that the good Lord had sent us the three boys to fill what would have been a great void in our lives.

With all the building going on around Tindale and Loppington, not only of housing estates but of shopping centers, my thoughts strayed towards the possibility of a builder making me an offer for our land.

I did not like to think what my father would have said to these thoughts, but, as a fair man, he would have understood that anything I did was for the best. He had had his life and now it was my turn and we must move with the times, and admit that farming was in decline.

Modern imports were taking the peoples fancy, after so much austerity.

In 1947 Princess Elizabeth, King George VI's eldest daughter, had married her Prince Charming Philip of Greece, and even she had to curtail her wedding celebrations. Women all over the country felt for her, and in sympathy, sent her some of their clothing coupons in order for her to purchase the necessary materials for her wedding dress.

The Monarch's way of thinking was that if the people have to be rationed then so must they. We heard they were also rigid in following the rule of water in the bath to ankle depth only.

On 31st January 1952 the princess, now a mother of two, and her husband the Duke of Edinburgh were wished Godspeed by her mother, Queen Elizabeth, and King George VI, her father as they waved them off from London airport, on a flight to Kenya, the first 'leg' of what was to be an extended tour of the Commonwealth.

Just six days later, on the 6th of February, her father passed away.

On the 7th of February, it was Queen Elizbeth II who returned to London airport to be met by her Prime Minister, Sir Winston Churchill.

The country went into mourning and everyone felt so sorry for the new queen, who looked so vulnerable, at the age of just 25, to be taking

on the mammoth task of sovereignty, a role

she was not born into.

The following year, on June 2nd 1953 she was

to be crowned in a glorious ceremony at

Westminster Abbey.

As that rather wet day dawned the first news,

we heard over the wireless was that Edmund

Hillary, along with his Sherpa, Tensing, had

become the first to reach the summit of Mount

Everest. Hillary was a New Zealander, and

New Zealand, a part of the British Empire,

which in turn meant our Queen was their

Queen. This being the case it made their triumphant achievement, a rather massive, not to be out done, coronation present.

It continued to rain on the procession, but the whole nation was warmed by the pictures of the rather ample figure of Queen Salute of Tonga, riding to and from the ceremony in an open carriage. I came to understand, years late, that this was because by her custom, to ride in a closed coach would have been an insulting gesture. Salute was a woman who also knew what it was like to have duty thrust upon her at an early age, she was just eighteen when she became Queen of Tonga.

Tonga, a small island in the Pacific, I admit that I'd never heard of it, but we were also informed that the people of that island, had paid for three spitfires to be built to help in the war effort.

Some lucky people were able to watch the unfolding events on their new television sets, for many people had bought one in time for the occasion.

Those who did have sets invited neighbours, relatives or friends to join them. But wherever people were watching, or with ears glued to the wireless, everyone wished Her Majesty Queen Elizabeth II a long and happy life, 'Long to reign over us, God Save the Queen,' was the loyal toast across the country.

On a personal note, an amusing thing that happened between Helen and I. She pointed out to me that Prince Philip had knelt before his wife and promised to be her liege lord. 'What about you?' she asked, as she placed a cushion on the floor before her. I pointed out to her that Philip did not kneel before his wife he knelt before his Queen.

Apart from that, I said my wife's name is Helen, not Elizabeth. We had a chuckle, and she gave me a dig in the ribs hard.

Seven years later, in the spring of 1960, I felt that I had had enough of farming and craved a more normal life. The trouble was that farming was in my blood and I was finding it almost impossible to make a final decision.

I constantly wavered. Should I? Shouldn't I, Will I, Won't I.

Then the decision was taken out of my hands in the nature of a compulsory purchase order. They were planning on building a new dual carriageway straight through the middle of my farm.

They gave me two years' notice in which to sort out all my affairs.

Although I had been dithering about trying to come to a decision, I resented the fact that any decision I wished to make had now been taken completely out of my hands.

A very unreasonable reaction on my part, under the circumstances. No

Eventually the two years were up. I was duly compensated and had sold all, but my 'worldly goods.' These we had transferred to a small croft we had bought on the coast. I was retired, with money in the bank, and at the reasonably young age of fifty-three I felt that if

we played our cards right Helen and I could

enjoy a life of relative ease. No more working

all hours, in all weathers, what a blessing.

Billy's Wartime Farm

Chapter Seventeen

Helen and I settled into the slower life of the croft. Hard, was not now part of our vocabulary, but work, still was.

We could no way sit out all our days doing nothing, that was why we had bought a croft.

A picturesque little thatched roof cottage with a small acreage surrounding it, just enough for us to manage without breaking into a sweat.

We grew most of our own vegetables, potatoes, carrots, cabbage and such like, this then, was my domain.

Helen had me build a henhouse for her and a small chicken run. We very rarely had roast chicken on our menu though, unless the chicken came from the local butcher, as Helen had given all our hens names, so to eat them would be like eating a member of the family or so she said, but we did have plenty of eggs and she kept her hand in making bread and cakes.

By this time all our boys, Alfie, Georgie and Bobby were all in the forces. Alfie seemed a confirmed bachelor, Georgie had married a nice girl, Nancy, from Tindale and they had a small cottage there, close to Nancy's parents so she wouldn't feel lonely while Georgie was away. To our absolute joy, Nancy was pregnant and we looked forward to our first grandchild, and Helen was sending sparks flying from her knitting needles once again. Bobby was still playing the field, looking for Miss Right, or so he said, although we did notice the name of a certain Corporal Ruth Lloyd came into his conversation quite a lot. All three loved the area where the croft was situated, Alfie said he would like a place just like it when he retired from the army, and Bobby asked us to keep our eyes on the property market for him. They had grown up as country boys, and despite their travels with the Forces, they were still country boys.

Going back to my 'old stomping ground' to pay a visit to my parent's grave, I bumped into Ernie. It was unexpected on my part because I knew that he did not have relatives 'resting' there.

So, imagine my surprise when I saw him walking through the graveyard carrying flowers.

He explained that he had been successful in his search for answers surrounding Martin.

Apparently, Martin was part of a bomb disposal unit.

And as such was cleaning up unexploded bombs and landmines that had been 'planted' by the enemy. At one point, just before Martin was to prepare himself to disarm a device, he walked away, towards some trees, saying that he would only be 'two ticks.' His mates laughed at him, taking the mickey, assuming he was going, as it was politely said, to relieve himself. Very shortly after they heard an explosion and Martin never returned when his 'two ticks' were up. They never saw him again and assumed that either he had stepped on a mine and was blown to smithereens, or, as one fellow said, 'Either that or he'd lost his

nerve and scarpered, gone A.W.O.L.'

They found nothing of him, not even his 'dog

tally' to show that he'd been there, and so

therefore could not prove, one way or the

other, what had happened to him.

Sometime after they had left the farm to be

married, the Ministry of Defense had returned

Martin's personal belongings to the sisters,

with, at that time the notice of   missing,

presumed killed.

The sisters, not having any more of an

explanation, still held out hope.

Eventually, Ernie through due diligence, had traced an old buddy of Martins and he had told him all he knew of the matter. So, the twins had officially accepted he was dead and they buried his personal belongings in a grave and erected a headstone with the following epitaph 'Was lost, but is now found.'

No one who knew Martin, ever thought that he was capable of going absent without leave. Apart from his self-discipline and loyalty to his friends in the army, we knew there was not a 'cat in hell's chance' that he would leave his sisters in limbo causing them such distress deliberately.

144

I became very emotional when I realized just where that grave was situated.

Part of our farm had been turned over to the church to enable the graveyard to be extended, and Martin's grave backed on to where the old cowman's hut had stood.

Martin had truly returned home, if not in body, then most certainly in spirit.

Ernie and I spent the rest of the day in each other's company. We called in to the local pub for a pint and 'chewed the fat' together for what seemed like hours. He told me that he had never married his gentle widow lady from all those years ago. It seems that survivors' guilt got the better of both of them, surviving while their partners had not. Even though this was the case they still kept each other company, still 'tripping the light fantastic' at the tea dance right up until her illness prevented it and she had passed away because of that illness just four months before our meeting. On returning home to the croft, I told Helen all about my meeting up with Ernie, that he had told me what he had found out about Martin. Helen wept a little at my news and finally   let Martin go. Finally accepting that he would never be coming home.

I also told her that I thought the loss of the gentle widow lady had taken a great toll on Ernie's health, that to me he had not looked at all well.

It was not long after we heard that Ernie had also died after a short illness.

I returned once again to Tindale for Ernie's funeral and my heart was glad, when I saw so many people attend the service. We met many of the people who had been workers on the farm. A very spritely woman with purple hair came and introduced herself to us. "You don't remember me, do you?" she said. "Can't blame you. I used to be one of those fit young

Land Army Girls working your farm during the war," "Changed a bit, haven't I?"

We met up again with Martin's sister Joan who told us that Mary was away visiting in laws in America. We met Pavel, her husband, and their young son, Paul, which we guessed was English for Pavel.

We also met a young man who said that his dad had come from Krakow in Poland and his mum had been one of the Timber Girls who worked locally, they had met at the sawmills. It seems he had heard many stories of the prominent locals and read about Ernie in the obituary column. Ernie would have been

'tickled.'

It was so very nice to catch up with people with

whom we had been through so much, many of

us having to grow old heads on young

shoulders very quickly, during those war years.

 Lovely to share old stories of 'Do you

remember when, and 'Do you remember who.

But most of all it was so lovely to see so many

come to pay their last respects to Ernie, a

stalwart of the old community.

At this juncture, Helen and I took stock of our lives. We decided that even though we loved the croft, it was rather tying, and there were so many things in the world that we wanted to do and see before we grew past it.

The boys were settled in their lives. Our Georgie was now out of the army and working as a Farm Estate Manager for one of the landed gentries, he still loved the outdoor life. He and Nancy now had a daughter and a son, Suzie and 'Little Alfie.'

Little Alfie, after his uncle, who was now amusingly referred to as Big Alfie.

These two little ones were the apple of their Nana's eye, as well as mine.

Bobby was now married to Corporal Ruth Lloyd and were living in married quarters. They both wanted to spend more time in the Forces as they were loving the overseas postings. Both of the boys seemed happy with their partners, thank God, for so many marriages did not seem to be lasting the test of time as they had in the old days, and Suzie and Alfie were a bonus that neither Helen nor I could have ever imagined as we started out in married life. We also secretly looked forward to babies from daughter in law Ruth though we knew their decision not for some time, yet.

 Alfie had decided that he was definitely a confirmed bachelor and was still in the Army, now having risen through the ranks to that of Sergeant Major.

Christmases were now, once again, a great pleasure, with the boys, their wives and grandchildren gathered around us. Our home was alive once again with the laughter of children and by the grace of God long may it continue.

Now was the time, I told Helen, to make out

what I called our 'Things to do List.'

To make a list of things we had missed out on,

and while our health still held, and we had

brass in the bank, we could, and should,

indulge ourselves. Starting with a honeymoon

that was well, put off so many times for so

many reasons over the years, except the few

days we had in   not the very best hotel, but a

good one in Loppington, all those years ago.

Helen said, with brass in the bank she was not

going on what used to be the traditional

weekend in Blackpool, she fancied a trip on

that train which that Belgian detective in the

Agatha Christie books, went on and solved a

murder The Orient Express, no less.

Billy's Wartime Farm

Chapter Eighteen

After working so hard all my life the journey on the Orient Express was an opulent episode in our lives talk about how the other half live. We absolutely enjoyed ourselves to the maximum and were thankful that there was no need for a Monsieur Poirot. The journey was smooth, the scenery spectacular, the food out of this world, everything was pure luxury.

We returned home and settled into our new role of retirees; we weren't old enough yet to be called pensioners.

It was so good to be able to do things at our own pace, at a time that suited us not anyone else. Healthwise, we were not too badly off, apart from the odd aches and pains expected in old age. As that great star of the Golden Age of Hollywood, Bette Davis, was reported to have said, 'Old age is not for wimps.' How right she was. But sitting around doing nothing was not in my remit.

I had long had an ambition to write a story. Stories I understand should contain love, happiness, a few tears and maybe some melodrama, so what better than to write the story of my life.

My life had love and happiness in it, thinking of my love for Helen and the joy the boys brought to us, followed by the little ones, plus our joint love of the land.

It had sorrow in it, just think of all the sadness that the war years brought. Not to mention the passing of so many, much loved family members and dear friends.

It had drama, bringing to mind the night we watched the fires from Liverpool, and that German bomber that came down not far from our village.

It had laughter in it, apart from the laughter

and happy times within my own family I was

thinking of the villagers trying their best to

communicate with the Polish refugees,

speaking their native English but opening their

mouths wide, speaking more slowly, loudly,

and gesticulating a lot, as if that made any

difference to someone who had never been

out of their own country until they ended up in

Wales.

It had pathos, when I thought about old Ernie

and his gentle widow lady who would not

marry because she felt guilty about her new

found happiness.

Tragedy, well, we were surrounded by tragedy from 1939 to 1946, thinking especially of Martin, but we kept on going. So I reckoned that as far as a book was concerned, my life had all the ingredients.

Writing would be my reason to get up in the morning, for I had seen too many people retire and then waste away from sheer boredom, not to mention there was always our 'Things to Do List' to keep my mind focused.

The to do's Helen was adding to it were becoming beyond a joke and sometimes downright scary. Wing walking, sky diving, snorkeling, where did she get the ideas from, I suspected too many Hollywood movies.

When I read the list, I told her I thought she was having me on, if not, then she was on her own with those three. But, I said, she was in with half a chance of seeing the Eiffel Tower, the Aurora Borealis, and the Norwegian Fjords, but the Taj Mahal in India, was a flight too far.

When I took up the pen, or in my case, pencil, I could lose myself for hours reminiscing and scribbling down notes, in my many pads, on times and places long gone by. I would vaguely be aware that Helen had called me for lunch and I would answer just two minutes and I would turn up at the table to eat my stone-cold soup about half an hour later. I became

so engrossed in my project. She would tut

and heave great sighs, but she knew that

when I wanted to do something I threw myself

into it wholeheartedly, for as my old friend

Ernie used to say if a thing's worth doing, it's

worth doing well. Besides as I pointed out to

Helen, writing as a habit, was not nearly so

bad as drinking, smoking, gambling, or finding

myself another woman, at which point Helen

flicked me, playfully, across the ear with the

tea towel and told me that as a punishment for

such a remark I was in sole charge of the

drying of the dishes for a week.

It did not seem to me at the time that Helen was taking my new hobby very seriously, but what I did not know was that whenever I went out for a walk, she would read what I had written, and secretly do sketches and drawings to use as illustrations in my book when it was finished.

Somewhere along the line we decided that as we had already 'honeymooned' on the Orient Express from our 'Things to do List and I categorically refused to go wing walking, we compromised and went to Blackpool for our wedding anniversary.

After loading up the car, Helen said she would take the first stint of driving.

As I climbed into the passenger seat, I noticed a box file on the back seat and expressed my curiosity. Helen said it was not a secret, but a surprise and invited me to have a look at the items in the file while she drove along, what a surprise I had.

She then confessed to me that each time I left the house she had read all I had written and had been making illustrations to suit the writing that I had done.

They were good, I had no idea that my wife had this hidden talent. She in turn said she

had no idea that I could write and express
myself so well.

We complimented each other, but we always
had, all are lives.

This time, like on the farm we would complete
the project together.

Can you imagine, there we were, after all
those years, discovering something new about
each other, that was a good item for anybody's
'Things to Do List.'

Set about find something out about each other
that we didn't already know.

But not hopefully of new discoveries about
each other.

This book was inspired by and written in tribute to,

the veterans, ex service personnel, staff and

volunteers of the Veteran Centre,

Molyneaux House, School Lane, Scholes, Wigan.

I wish also to dedicate it the men and women, who

lost their lives fighting for are freedom and libertys.

Especially for

2770433 Sergeant Thomas Brighouse,

1st Battalion Irish Guards,

Killed in action. 30th April 1943

Aged 27. No known grave.

Medjez El Bab Memorial

Face 13

Tunisia. North Africa.

Other books written by this author:

Stonehaven Manor.

Stonehaven Manor The War Years.

Stonehaven Manor The Post War Years.

Stonehaven Manor The Dowager.

Stonehaven Manor The Retirement.

The Three Grandmas' Nature Reserve.

Me Owd Fettler.

Simmsburgh Castle

Wyvern House.

Th' Owd Rugged Church.

Yew tree farm

Printed in Great Britain
by Amazon

22271667R00096